MARY'S ENGLISH GENTLEMAN

Bonanza Brides Find Prairie Love Series Book 6

KAT CARSON

RoyceCardiff
Publishing House
WHOLESOME INSPIRATIONAL ROMANCE

RoyceCardiff
Publishing House
WHOLESOME INSPIRATIONAL ROMANCE

CONTENTS

A PERSONAL WORD FROM KAT

I love writing about the old West and the trials, tribulations, and triumphs of the early pioneer women.

With strong fortitude and willpower, they took a big leap of faith believing in the promised land of the West. It was always not a bed of roses, however many found true love.

Thank you for being a loyal reader.

Kat

Bonanza Brides Find Prairie Love Series
Book 1 Secret's
Book 2 Robbed
Book 3 Broken Love
Book 4 The School Master
Book 5 Vagabond Heart
Book 6 Mary's English Gentleman
Book 7 The Lost Bride

PROLOGUE

MARY BROWN HAD LIVED ON THE EDGE SINCE SHE'D been ten. It had been her Pa who'd taught her how to con people out of an earnest living. She wasn't as naïve as to think that she could keep getting away with it, that she'd never get caught, but thirteen years later, it was more a terrible habit, an addiction, than anything else.

Later in life, Mary found she would have liked to erase that part of her life, iron out the folds, leave all the bruises out. But if things hadn't happened the way they were supposed to happen, then she supposed Mary Brown wouldn't have been Mary Brown at all.

The thing about life was, you never knew where it went. Whether it went right, or wrong, or took some really twisted turns on the carousal of fate. She wondered if her parents had known what path she might take in life, and still loved her unconditionally for it.

She still wondered if she could go back in time and stop herself from carrying out that first con.

THE FIRST TIME SHE'D STARED INTO THE WRINKLY EYES of a kindly faced woman, she'd been genuinely starving, and she'd found out that people tended to give more easily if they believed you showed them your vulnerable side. The side with the ugly, dirty face, mud caked onto your cheeks, knees freshly bruised and bleeding.

She still remembered how the woman had gasped when she'd found her hiding with a loaf of bread behind the wash buckets, scandalized that a small rascal of a child would actually dare commit thievery in a place as sacred as her bakery. Then Mary had turned, fully intending to shove past the lady, and book it out of there, to find somewhere safe and wait for her Pa to come back.

But for just a second, their eyes had met, and she'd seen the shock of her existence actually register in the back of that woman's mind – the scraggly looking hoodlum shaking with hunger and skittish with desperation.

She'd seen the war in that woman's eyes. Did she hand her over to the Sherriff, or take pity on the small child?

In the end, sympathy won over a desire for retribution, because what would have been the meaning of retribution when a starving child was punished for an act of desperation?

Mary had seen the exact moment her compassion had won out. The woman had let out a long winded sigh, rubbed at her eyes, and crouched down in front of her. Back then she'd been terrified. She knew that she would have to go home, to a place where they'd just buried Ma's dead body in the back yard, and she knew that Pa must have been frantic with worry. But she didn't want to go, didn't want to see, and didn't want to live without her Ma.

So when the woman had reached out and put a kindly hand on her small arm, she'd actually cringed away. She'd thought about that terrible disease that had made her Ma cough blood, and been terrified that it would take her Pa away too. When the lady had looked at her with that sorry sort of commiseration, Mary had wanted nothing more than to sink into that grave as well and be held in her Ma's loose embrace.

In the end, she'd been gently cast out in the back alley with a warning and a long loaf of bread. She'd been so relieved, and her chest had bubbled with so much sorrow, that without knowing, without realizing, she'd trudged all the way up the foot of a hill and found herself standing in front of their small shanty.

Pa had sat waiting on the porch with a harried look on his face. She still wondered what would have happened had she never returned, had the kind lady offered her a bit more refuge, had she lost her way and never found it back.

The 'what if's' were strange, and some of them made

her heart clench because maybe, just *maybe*, her life would have been completely different.

HER PA HAD BEEN A CLOTH MERCHANT, AND CLAIMED TO have the best quality silks and chiffons that lassies would ever get their hands on. Her Ma had been a seamstress of immense talent, and together, her Ma and Pa had run a business that would have failed without each other.

Mary still remembered how those pretty gowns glinted in the dim light of their lantern. The rose golds, the powder blues, the glossy greens, the poufy skirts and their frou-frou accoutrements. She remembered secretly running her hands through the silks, marveling at their softness. She remembered the rough texture of the crochet, and she distinctly remembered wanting to be big enough to try one of those gowns herself.

She remembered the put-putting of her Ma's sewing machine, the steady rhythm of the thread seaming into the cloth, the magic of plain pieces of cloth coming together to make the most beautiful of clothes.

"I want to make one too," she remembered telling her Ma one day.

Ma, who'd been concentrating with furrowed brows on a particularly tricky sleeve joint, had suddenly looked up and squinted at her. "Really?"

Mary remembered her Ma as a tall woman with a slim, beautiful face, and kind brown eyes. In retrospect, she'd been golden haired and green eyed, with a round face and cutting cheekbones, not unlike her Pa's. Where her Ma was beautiful in a soft, unadorned, unembellished sort of way, Mary was all glamour and allure, even when she was a young child. "She'll grow up to be a beautiful young lass," people used to tell her parents.

But in the back of her mind, all she'd ever wanted to be was tall and simple, like her Ma. She wanted to have those kind eyes and that pretty, but not beautiful, smile. When her ma had squinted questioningly at her that day, her eyes had glittered with something dark and smoldering. Maybe it had been gleeful passion about her daughter finally resembling her for once, in one single aspect, but when Mary had nodded yes, her Ma's smile had been almost blinding.

And so she'd been assigned to construct proper proportions on stray pieces of clothes, cut them in proper ratios, and sew small frocks for her dollies by hand. She spent her afternoons with Pa, looking through rich textures and learning about clothes, and the evenings with her Ma, huddled up in the crook of her side, patiently sewing clothes for her dollies and enjoying the warmth of her Ma's embrace.

Life had been good then, and sometimes she still found solace in the comfort of those memories.

But then, two years later, when she'd just turned nine, her Ma had caught the disease. Tuberculosis the medical man had called it. It has started out as a regular old annual fever with a light cough, which no one had paid much mind to. How Mary wished to go back in time and warn her younger self. If only she'd known. It was an intense yearning of wanting to get something precious back, of wanting to be small and comfortable in the warmth of her Ma's embrace.

Things had escalated quickly once the initial diagnose

had been confirmed. Ma had slowly become wrought with long fits of coughing that had drained her once they subsided. Mary had been barred from entering her room without supervision for her Pa's fear of her catching the disease. So, she'd watched from the very periphery as her Ma slowly lost all color, all strength, as her face became pale and drawn out, as her hair started falling away, as her lips became rough and red by coughing too much blood, how she slowly lost that sparkle in her eyes.

After five long months of watching one of the most important people in her life lose herself, it finally happened.

Her Ma passed away.

THE BROWNS HAD NEVER BEEN PARTICULARLY RELIGIOUS people. They didn't aggrandize their religion, but in the quiet of their home, Mary had always been taught the Holy Book. How hardships defined the kind of human you eventually became, how God was always there in the smallest of things when you needed Him the most, and how His love for his creation defied logic and convictions.

Corinthians 16:14. Let all that you do, be done in love.

It was Mary's favorite verse. She kept it tucked close to her heart when Pa would scold her, or Ma would throw her a slightly disapproving glance. It kept her grounded, even when she was a young lass, because she knew that she loved her Ma and Pa, the clothes, and the sewing more than she could ever actually put in words.

She said quiet prayers before every meal, and thanked God for each day before she went to bed. When Ma fell sick, she used to stay up all night praying for miracles that would never come.

When Ma passed away, she remembered questioning her beliefs, remembered lying awake in the night, staring up at the ceiling, through the ceiling, looking at the infinity where God lived, and asking silently in her mind, in her heart, why He had to take her Ma away.

Maybe it had been that crack in her faith, or maybe it had been the crack in her heart, but in the back of her mind, in every dusty, hidden corner of her heart, she attributed that nick for where her life led her astray.

2

PA'S MERCHANDISING HAD BECOME FAMOUS. HE OFFERED excellent cloth, along with the prime services that people were looking for. Her Ma's talent as a seamstress had been beyond par. Her skirts had that inherently poufy outlook that lassies could only achieve by fixing down a mesh layer of gauze, and ladies loved how each seam was so intrinsic that it never really showed.

They had been a team, her Ma, and Pa. In so many ways, her Ma had been her Pa's lucky charm.

If her Ma had been simple and subdued, then her Pa had been golden and full of bright, happy light. He loved with all that he had, and never held anything back. Loud and boisterous, he had hoards of friends, who had been one of the many reasons their merchandising métier had spread by word of mouth. She would later learn that having connections, the *right* connections, in the world of business was an important aspect.

They'd never had to live a hard life in the Great Plain, as many of the farmers and other Barnstead's were bound to do, but she'd never known an excess in wealth either. It had been a perfect balance of having something, saving it, and earning more. Her Ma and Pa did good business, and though she'd never been donned in layers of gold or diamonds, she'd always been comfortable.

But when Ma had gotten sick, all the savings had been pooled into providing the best care for her. The medical man had asked for an ample amount of money to acquire the best of medicine, and because their business was as much a family, and vice versa, the merchandising had to stop for a while. There had been no new earnings, the savings had dried up, and in the end, Mary and her Pa had been left with nothing but a raging grief, and bitter regrets when Ma had passed away.

❦

PA HAD HAD A TENDENCY TO BOAST ABOUT HOW HE provided the best fabric for the clothes that his wife sewed, and as the business had expanded, their merchandise had been in want by ladies of old and new wealth alike.

Maybe he'd been telling the truth before, but Mary knew that the fabric he'd been selling in the three months of her Ma's illness had been bought and haggled for at the local market. However, her Pa had never missed a beat as he'd smiled the biggest, most sincere smile behind the haggard looking scruff of his beard and boasted about how his fabric was the best of the best, and there was nothing like it to be found elsewhere on the Great Plain.

Unknowingly, she's taken note, and compartmentalized the sheer confidence that her Pa exuded despite the lies.

How he held his shoulders straight and confident, how his grin never wavered, how his eyes never shifted, and how his feet never shuffled.

And when the ladies queried about his wife, he'd wave away their worries with a swift movement of his hand and say, "She'll be up an' runnin' in a few days," with such utter confidence that even Mary, who'd had a front row seat to her Ma's slow digression, would tend to believe it.

She knew that it had been those moments when she'd taken to lying. Apparently conning people for her own benefit ran in her blood, and who was she to sway past genetics?

SHE DIDN'T QUITE KNOW WHY SHE STARTED DOING WHAT she did, but she did know that there was a certain satisfaction in going for what you wanted, and actually *getting* it.

There were exactly three bakeries in the little town that she and her Pa lived in, and when they had no money, and no food on the table, it was Mary who'd taken it upon herself to improvise for the sake of survival. It had been hard on her, on her hear and her soul, to stake out the bakery, to sit behind the bushes and observe as the people went in and came out with wonderful smelling pastries.

Her mouth had watered, and her knees had throbbed.

She'd waited until a time had come when the small shop had been empty, then gotten up and carefully taken off her hooded cloak. Underneath, she'd worn the best frock that she'd owned at that time, a rose princess cut with a flowing skirt, and her hair had been teased into a golden halo. It had taken several hours of experimenting with the animal brush to get that look, and when she looked in the mirror, a sufficient amount of rogue on her cheeks rendered her if not entirely, then quite strangely, in a noble sort of way.

So, at ten and a half, as she strode inside the bakery with a hammering heart and a concaving stomach, it had been misery that had propelled her to smile like the most radiant beam of the sun and say, "I'm gonna have a bag full o' tarts."

The baker, a middle aged man with crow's feet around his eyes, had looked at her strangely.

"Are you alone?" he'd asked her, looking around, then squinting at her to get a better look.

She'd puffed up her cheeks to seem appropriately angry. "My Mama's in the carriage outside."

The man craned his neck to look outside the glass shop window.

Mary's heart thundered.

A customer walked into the shop.

Taking that distraction to count, she petulantly stomped her foot on the floor and glared at the man. He seemed taken aback, but she was emulating an emotionally dysfunctional, ill-mannered child, and her insides were burning with starvation, and she wanted so *desperately* to eat those tarts.

Another set of customers showed up and Mary pretended to pout, but those were actual tears brimming in her eyes. *Please*, she prayed. *Just this once*.

And even though she'd refused to count on God, He must have still loved her, because the next moment the man was shrugging and loading up a bag with tarts. He handed it to her, and she instantly took out one, ate it like a deprived rascal who hadn't eaten in days, and when the shop was flowing with more customers the baker could handle, she sneaked out, gathered her cloak, and ran as fast as she could.

She wanted to feel terrible because she'd essentially just stolen from an innocent man, but the tears flowing down her cheeks were that of gratitude. That her stomach had finally stopped gnawing on itself, and that her Pa, who'd been lying down in a miserable heap all day, would finally get something to eat.

When she presented him with a plateful, he didn't ask where she'd gotten them. He'd looked away, refusing to meet her eyes, and she'd watched his shoulders shake with silent tears as took one of the tarts, and ate it.

She'd cried right along with him.

＊ 3 ＊

THERE HAD BEEN AN INCIDENT. WELL, *SEVERAL* incidents, one after the other, growing worse in succession, as if amplified like a snowball rolling down a hill.

A few days after Ma had died, Mr. Aldridge, whose wife was one of Pa's regular customers, came to pay them a visit, and not of the nice, sympathetic variety. Mary didn't know what exactly went down behind the closed doors of Pa's small parlor, but she did stick close enough to realize that that thumping and crashing from inside was of someone getting beaten.

Later she would realize that he'd been caught. Her Pa, who'd been so adamantly lying about his business, about the quality of the fabrics, and selling them at an obscenely high price to pay for the treatment of his dying wife, had been found out, and no charming smiling, or regretful situation could have saved him from a terrible beat down.

She remembered putting a cool cloth to his swollen cheek that evening, how he'd held her to his side and wailed. It had been heartbreaking.

Maybe she should have taken caution from her father's rather brutal end, but she'd needed to survive, and taking things from right under people's noses had been the only thing she'd been good at.

She could have become a seamstress, but no one wanted to hire the daughter of the town fraud, especially when the rumor mill had kicked into high gear. "His daughter is jus' the same! She took a right amount of bread from right underneath my nose!"

And so, she and her Pa picked up the fragmented pieces of their lives, and moved away.

SOUTH DAKOTA WAS A LANDLOCKED STATE, AND IN THAT state were a lot of small towns. Pa's infamy preceded him in the fabric merchandising market, and in every town they lived in, Mary took up a job as a seamstress apprentice, built a solid network of connections with the townsfolk, and when no one was suspecting, donned the 'innocent' angel charisma. She took fleet from right under the townsfolk noses until rumors started to spread again, and they had no choice but to flee.

On and on it went, from Deadwood to Dallas, until she didn't even feel the smallest morsels of remorse while taking from others.

From Montana to Wyoming, she and her Pa became a tag team of cons, taking advantage of people and giving nothing in turn until the entirety of her heart was nothing but a hardened bit of coal.

Mary would have liked playing the innocent seamstress card, but as she reached adolescence, her body started changing. By the time she turned sixteen, it became frustratingly harder to blink her big green eyes and get whatever she'd want.

But as one door closed, another one opened.

She'd never been terribly fond of her inherent beauty. She'd always wanted to exchange her flowing golden hair with her mother's brown mane, her cutting green eyes for warm brown ones, but in the end, it had been that beauty which had saved her from a depressingly low key situation.

It happened first when she'd been sitting in the town square, head in her hands, heart in her throat, not knowing what to do next because she'd just been evicted from the tailor shop for having been trying to sneak out a pair of scissors.

So carried away had she been in her despair that she'd never noticed when a young man of a rather sunny disposition sat just beside her.

"Hello there, lassie," he'd said in a voice that was equal parts cheery and warm.

She'd slowly turned around, carefully examining his face. He was tan, with enormous cerulean eyes that crinkled with the force of his smile.

"Mind tellin' me yer' name?" he'd asked.

She'd picked up her skirt and stood up abruptly, feeling a warm flutter in her chest, something that had made her panic beyond belief because never had she felt like that. Her panic might have showed in her face, because instantly the man's grin had dropped into a frown, and he'd held out his arms in defense.

"Whoa, whoa. Calm down, lass. I promise I ain't a lecher."

Which hadn't really eased her pounding heart, and she'd thought rather nastily, *How would I know?*

She'd pursed her lips, turned on her heel, and whirled around, fully intending to stride away–

And had caught her foot on a fist size pebble and fallen smack on her face.

He'd been there to help her up, and when her hand had touched his palm, she'd felt curious tingles. She'd promptly snatched them away, cheeks warming, looking anywhere but at him, and mumbled a distinctly ungrateful sounding "Thanks".

He'd grinned, shining like the halo of the sun, and rubbed a hand on the back of his neck. "I'm Nate," he told her in a bright, warm tone.

Nate had walked her all the way to the door of the terrible looking shanty that they'd rented out, and didn't said an unkind word when she refused to invite him in.

The next day, he'd been standing outside her door when she'd left to look around town for a job. He'd stepped off the dingy rails and shot her a brilliant smile. Mary had walked right past him, and he'd followed.

He'd accompanied her around town, and so golden had he been, that the townsfolk had lined around to bask in his glow. Within a day he'd gotten Mary a spot at a small tailoring shop at the very edge of the town, because even with golden boy at the helm, only so many people were willing to hire a thief.

In the end, Lauren had given up erecting an icebound wall around herself, and had been genuinely moved when she thanked him – this time from the heart.

And thus had started her very odd, very awkward courtship with Nathanial Headway. Two weeks into their young love, she'd been summoned to the Headway Estate, where she'd been greeted by a frumpy looking woman in her forties. She'd had that 'just come into some new money' look about her, and she looked down on Mary with such derision that it made Mary's heart flame.

The burning was only intensified when she'd been splashed in the face with a glass of water. Mary had had to count several heartbeats to calm herself down. It was only the displacement of being in an enemy territory, and Nate's bright smile in her mind that had stopped her from getting up and ripping the woman to shreds with her bare hands.

"I want ye' te' leave my son alone," the woman had ordered.

Mary bristled. "An' what if I *won't?*"

The woman had smiled grimly. "Then ye' better prepare fer' the consequences, girl."

Mary had rode off that Estate on a high horse, and righteous indignation.

The very next day, she'd lost her job.

A day after, the townsfolk had started giving her the side eye.

Three days after, everyone had started avoiding her like the plague.

Nate had noticed, been by her side through it all, but even his bright, optimistic charm hadn't managed to cast away her gloom. She'd been angry, furious, so full of rage that she'd demanded he talk to his mother on her behalf, to which Nate had shamefully bowed his head.

"She'll come around," he'd told Mary, and she'd bristled,

feeling her heart, which had been slowly shedding its dark in the light of Nate's glow, harden up again.

Maybe Nate had noticed, because in an act of defiance and desperation, he'd asked her to elope with him.

In a fit of cold fury, Mary had agreed.

However, she'd known that the Halstead's would never accept her. If worst came to worse, they'd cast both Mary and Nate out on the streets, and for a boy like Nate, living like Mary would be the worst kind of affront. He wouldn't survive.

She didn't want that for him. She didn't want that for herself.

And so she camped in front of the estate for half a day before a tenant showed her to the main house where Nate's Ma waited with a smirk on her face.

Mary had come prepared with an arsenal. If she couldn't have Nate, then she would walk out this situation with something that would help her survive in the world outside. With a smirk of her own, she'd sat in front of Mrs. Halstead with a confidence that she hadn't had before, because this time she had nothing to lose, and everything to gain, and she needed that pseudo confidence to play this right.

"Ye' willin' te' give up my boy, lass?" Mrs. Halstead asked delicately.

"Ye' willin' te' give somethin' in turn fer' yer' boy?" Mary asked in turn.

Apparently, Mrs. Halstead had been expecting complete and utter surrender, not a negotiation. She sputtered, and Mary took that as cue to set out her conditions.

"Ye' give me expenses fer' travel, a carriage with two

horses, and a trunk full of clothes, an' I'll be away from here as soon as possible."

Mrs. Halstead had been catching up with her situation by now, and she seemed to have been pretty angry about it. "An' if I don'?"

Mary leaned back in her chair, and smiled very smugly. "Did'ja know Nate proposed te' me?"

Mrs. Halstead had recoiled, looking scandalized.

"I'm gonna marry him," Mary went on. "And when yer' family casts us out, I'm gonna drag him to the pits with me."

Mrs. Headway looked like she was about to have an aneurysm. Eye wide, nose flaring, and with a short breath, she gasped out, "And what will' ye do once ye' get all ye' ask fer?"

Mary smiled grimly. It pained her to say what she was about to do, but she also knew that Nate needed a dose of reality. He was soft and bright and used to getting his way. There was no place for someone like that in the world she lived in. He would drag her down, and she would kill the sparkle in his eyes.

So, she said, "I would break his heart."

Mrs. Headway frowned, and Mary shrugged.

"He won't ever go against his Mama, again. Isn't tha' what ye' want?"

Mrs. Headway seemed to actually worry about him for a few moments. She chewed on her lip, looked shifty, and less mean and intimidating than she'd been just a few minutes ago.

Then, she sighed and mumbled, "I'm doin' this fer' his own good."

And the deal was sealed.

WHEN MARY ACCEPTED THE RING NATE OFFERED HER that day, she had no intention of actually showing up at the altar. She watched his back as he disappeared around the corner, and prayed for forgiveness about what she was about to do.

She knew he'd wait for her all night long, and when he would realize that she wasn't going to show up, he would gear up to look for her. She needed to disappear before that happened.

But for just a single moment, she allowed herself to fall down and break. She sat on the ground, buried her head in her arms, cried silently, and lamented herself for being hard and vicious and jaded. In that moment, she wanted so bad to be charming and honest and truthful. She wanted to take back all those years of conning and sinning and wash herself anew.

For just those few minutes, she allowed herself to be miserable.

When she got up, her heart was sheathed in an armor of ice and cold. She walked all the way home, where her Pa stood at the edge of their shanty, staring in wonder at the tall, smooth carriage which waited at their doorstep.

The years had taken their toll on him. His once golden hair was now perpetually dirty and matted, his eyes were hollow, his mind dark. He seemed to have lost his will to live, and sometimes Mary thought the only thing that drove him to move from one place to another was his immense love for her. When he looked at Mary with a frown on his face, she wanted to run into his arms and stay wrapped in his embrace forever.

Even in the state he was in, he seemed to understand her terrible misery. He held his arms aloft, and without ever realizing the moments, or registering her surroundings, she ran to him. She felt warm when he hugged her close, and felt an overwhelming tightening of her chest when he mumbled into her hair, "It's gonna be okay, little girl. It's gonna be okay."

Mary almost believed him. After all those years, there was still conviction in his lies.

◈

BY AFTERNOON, THEY'D CLEARED MORE THAN HALF THE distance from the edge of Wyoming, and by the time they entered Montana, Mary's heart had felt a little less bruised. If the beginning of the day had been a sucker punch to her, then she could only imagine what Nate would have to go through that night.

In the end, she refused to think about it, distracting herself by counting out the money Mrs. Halstead had sent, and examined each and every crevice of the coach as her Pa drove the horses. It was top notch. Nate's Ma had paid in quality for her son's freedom.

She leaned back in the plush seat and sighed. After staring at the motion static roof for a good five minutes, she pulled out the ring. It was smooth and silver, with a tiny zircon gem on the top – maybe the only thing he could have afforded at the moment.

Her heart ached once more, but she forced her mind to plan ahead, to move forward.

She had to live. She had to survive.

❅   4   ❅

SURVIVAL TURNED OUT TO BE A KEY FACTOR IN RELATION to how she pulled what she now liked to call 'The Nate' on several more young lads. While liking Nate had been inherent, even congenital, Hardin, Montana was a hard town to survive in, and the years had taken away her will, as well as her desire, to work for an honest living.

Her short lived courtship with Nate had also taught her that she had an inborn beauty that attracted fine young men. Her hair how hung past her waist, her eyes were always make up so that the green of them shined bright, and her cheeks were touched up with a light shade of rouge that made them look cutting. With the trunk full of gowns Mrs. Headway had sent for her, she looked especially stunning.

So, when the handsome boy approached the new girl in town, she didn't shy away from him, and when she'd milked him for all he was worth, she ran away.

Slowly but steadily, her armoire grew, her possessions became more, and her heart became a lump of flesh that only beat to keep her alive. For years to come, she kept up the shenanigans. She's meet a new boy in each town, make him fall madly in love with her, make them give her all that they could offer in terms of material possessions, and when they popped up the ring, she would accept it and run away.

Like all good cons, there was always a great amount of reconnaissance involved. She mingled with the town ladies and figured out who was worth what, then strategically placed herself in their line of sight, waiting to be approached.

They *always* approached.

Then the game would begin. Shy away, be coy, tell the tragic back story, make them fall in love, make them give away all their worth, and when nothing but the altar was left, run away.

She heard about David Griffon via the Miles City grapevine. It was a town ahead of its time, with a full-fledged railway system, a thriving market, and a population of handsome young men. Mary rented out a cottage in the town's best residential district. Pa was getting sicker and weaker now. She knew there wasn't much time left for him, and she didn't know what she would do without him.

His stubble had grown out into a long, white beard, and he coughed in a way that reminded her eerily of the days when Ma had suffered from the disease. But she knew that this was just age, and the full weight of how wrong his daughter had turned out, catching up to him.

She wanted to make the last of his days comfortable, so she set out to work. Mrs. Travis, the next door neighbor, had a big heart, and an even bigger mouth. When she came over to greet Mary and her Pa, she was fed the town's juiciest gossip, along with a delicious apple pie.

When asked about her family, Mary doled out her 'tragic' past, which wasn't completely far off base. She told Mrs. Travis about how her Ma had died of the disease, how her Pa had fallen into a pit of depression, and how they'd managed to survive with a loving father-daughter bond, which had brought them this far.

"But he's sick now, too," said Mary, the ache in her heart not quite as false as her intentions.

"Ye' poor dear," said Mrs. Travis, blinking away tears from her kind, round eyes.

Mary patted her hand, then strategically lowered her eyes to seem more downcast, sober, demure, and solemn at the same time. "He jus' wants te' see me married off te' a good household."

"I can help with that!" said Mrs. Travis, suddenly jumping off from her chair, looking passionate and energetic.

"Really?" asked Mary, infusing her voice with an appropriate amount of desperation.

Mrs. Travis nodded eagerly. "There's this young boy in town. Very rich, very handsome, an' he's jus' put in an order for a mail order bride. Ye' should write to him!"

Mary, who'd completely lost track around the term 'mail-order-bride', forced a smile.

Mrs. Travis rambled on about how he lived on a huge estate with no one but his 'butler person' and three younger sisters, and she listened with one ear, silently rethinking her strategy. She wasn't looking to get married, she just needed a scapegoat to pull of another con and run as far away as she could. She thought about venturing into town to meet new people the next day, and let out a relieved breath when Mrs. Travis finally showed herself out.

When she came back to the kitchen, Pa was biting into a piece of apple pie.

She smiled. "Ye' up, ol' man."

Pa grinned, and for a moment, he looked young and charming again. But Mary knew better. The lines around his eyes never disappeared.

She helped herself to a piece too and savored the tarty taste for a few silent moments before Pa cleared his throat.

"Mary," he said, his voice serious and gravelly.

Her heart instantly started to gallop.

"This needs te' stop."

This needs te' stop. Just four simple words. Her Pa telling her to rethink the way she was living. She didn't know why her eyes suddenly started to brim with tears.

"Pa..."

"Mary, listen," he said, leaning over the table, setting the pie aside. "We both know I'm not gonna make it any further."

"Don't say that," she whispered, voice thick, eyes wet.

Pa only smiled. "I's the end o' the lane fer me, kid."

She blinked away the tears and swallowed, trying to be strong, unaffected, while inside her lungs shriveled. She took a few deep breaths, never breaking eye contact with Pa.

"Then, what am I s'pposed to do?"

Pa nodded and leaned back in his seat. "I heard tha' woman."

Instantly, Mary was on her guard. "No," she replied firmly, in a voice that brokered no argument.

"Mary, child, listen–"

"Pa, *no!*"

"Mary–"

She stood up, not wanting to hear what he wanted to say, not knowing if she could look into his eyes and deny him one more time. She had walked around the table when he caught her arm. His grasp was feeble, and she could've easily shook him away, but he was Pa, and he was dying, and what if this was the last time she ever saw him?

Heart in her throat, she slowly turned around and faced him.

His smile was tight, and his eyes were flat, and when he hobbled towards the chair with her arm in his grasp, she didn't have the heart to pull away.

"Listen, child," he said. "I have failed ye' in more ways than I would ever be able te' count."

"You haven't!" Mary insisted, as much admonishing as she rebuked. Pa was alive, all these years, and that had been more than enough.

"But it's time fer me te' go," he continued gently, as if he knew he was walking on thin ice and needed to tread carefully.

Mary's lip wobbled.

"An' I need te' make sure tha' I leave ye' in good hands."

"No one's hands are as good as yer's!"

Pa sighed, looking world weary and on the verge of collapse. "Jus'," he said, leaning back and holding his face in his hands, "do this one las' thing fer yer Pa. Please."

How could she have said no?

❧　5　❧

DAVID GRIFFON WAS WHAT THE LOCALS USED TO REFER as "The Remittance Man." He never quite got the hang of it. For seventeen years of his life, he'd lived in the Isles of the Great Kingdom. Britain. Before Britain itself had cast him out of her heart.

He still remembered the never-quite-sunny weather of his home, its tall monuments, great architecture, and even greater scenery. The stone walls, the elongated finials which touched the skies, and walking on cobblestoned paths amongst tight, lively streets.

Then he compared them to the stifling heat and uneven shanties of the 'Great' plain and felt his spirits lower.

The Hanoverian Succession had come about as a result of Act of Settlement, passed by the Parliament of England, which excluded Roman Catholics from succession. After the death of Queen Anne, and with no living children, David's cousin, five times removed, George I, had been the first in line for succession as one of the only heirs with no relations to the Roman Catholic Church.

Nevertheless, greed had conquered, and in an effort to remove any and all possible heirs from standing up or speaking out, the lot next in line had been collected and paid a huge sum of money in exchange for being shipped off to North America.

David had been one of those heirs. He hadn't known what had possessed his father to accept that money, but he knew that the circumstances must have been dire, for his father loved him and the triplets very much. So, he'd accepted the voyage to the American soil and promised his father he'd take care of everything, and maybe one day even return back home.

With much difficulty, he'd found a state close enough to give the illusion of home in Miles City, Montana. It had been a terrible move. The girls had cried for days, the people in town gave him uncanny looks, and Albert, his butler from back home, used foreign ingredients to cook meals that never tasted of home. He'd missed his father terribly, and had several inclinations to run away back home, to just take the girls, buy a ticket, and move it.

A month later his father had been assassinated, and though he'd been devastated enough to request access to the closest shipping route, that had been the day that he'd been completely cut off from his homeland.

With no father, and a mother who'd died during child-birth, David had nothing but himself and the triplets left of his life from before.

It had taken him a long time to get over the death of his father, and, to much extent, he'd never quite forgotten that vicious savagery. But he'd also had three young girls of age five to take care of, and so life had gone on.

Victoria, Alyssa, and Anna had been born one after the other in the month of April, and with their tiny fists and red hair, bright smiles and nearly identical faces, they'd become the apple of their brother's eyes since the moment he'd seen them. He was almost twenty-five now, and the girls were growing up.

Albert, his age old butler, had long since started to pass him hints about 'needing a female touch around the house, sir.' It was his sly way of sharing off household duties, David thought sullenly. The man was getting old, and would never admit to wanting a much needed vacation.

But there was a wise sort of forethought to those hints too, David knew. The girls were going to get older, and he wouldn't always know how to be there for them in all the ways that someone needed to be there for a growing young girl. If they had been back home, there would have been a plethora of housemaids and close friends, but as it were, they were permanently stranded in a strange land where people talked in twang-y drawls and half syllables, market places were short, brute affairs, and had the most awful taste in food he could imagine.

He didn't want to invite one of those women into his life, his home, and it made him cringe to even think about hearing his sisters speaking a half language that wasn't even their own.

"But, Sir," said Albert, neatly bowing his head when David confided in him. "This is all you have, and I may be stepping out of bounds, but this is what you *need* to do. You cannot be a recluse or else the girls would follow your lead, and–"

"I get it," David had snapped, feeling irritated because Albert was essentially right. He needed to conform to this place, if not for himself, then for the girls. It was basic animal instinct to acclimatize, he told himself, and very morosely, asked Albert for advice again.

"How do you expect me to go about this business, Albert?" he asked distastefully.

"Well, Sir," Albert began, then he'd hesitated. David knew he was about to be doomed. "You could always mingle with the town's ladies, and court one of them," Albert suggested tentatively, and David knew that there was more to come.

"Or?"

"Or," said Albert delicately, "you might use the local custom of ordering a bride."

The silence had been drawn out and awkward.

"*Order* a bride?" David had asked gingerly, cringing at the indelicacy of that thought. Such an inhumane custom of an inhumane land.

"Oh, it's not quite as brutish as it sounds, Sir."

"Really?" said David, voice dry as the desert.

"Really. You just... *endorse* yourself in the local newspaper, and... and the ladies would send you letters."

David shot him a bland look. "*Endorse* myself?"

Albert shrugged. "You could always try the conventional courting techniques, sir."

But he really didn't want to try the conventional courting techniques. That entailed that he go out and actively hunt for a woman to be his wife.

So, after careful deliberation, he *did*, in the end, endorse himself.

And the results were not half bad.

MARY HATED WHAT SHE WAS ABOUT TO DO. SHE HATED that she was even holding the pen to paper, and hated what she was about to write. She knew what endorsing herself in person was like. She knew well how to sell her charms, to make young lads knock each other away to have a chance with her.

But she didn't know what to *write* on that blank piece of paper.

Pa wanted her to marry that fool – and *stay* married.

She didn't want to do that, and she knew what to do so that this David Griffin would think the same.

So when she started writing, each word was the truth. She hadn't been completely honest in a full decade and more, and each stroke of pen on paper was like slashing her chest open, taking her heart out, and putting in on display. Her story was gritty and awful, designed to make even the most lecherous of men hate her. So she wrote about how she'd started out as a con, how she'd debilitated herself to God, and how she'd conned lots of men out of a living just so she and her Pa could survive.

She wanted David Griffin to take one look at her story and burn this letter, never to be heard from again.

And she would do that to anyone else who tried the same.

WITHIN TWO WEEKS OF HIS SELF-ENDORSEMENT, HE HAD a mailbox full of replies. From sixteen to thirty years old, each woman had attached a rather fetching picture of herself along with their replies.

"Oh, she's rather beautiful," said Victoria, skimming over the picture and looking impressed.

Anna snatched the picture and observed with a hawkish severity that a child her age shouldn't have been able to muster. In his lap, Alyssa cuddled close.

David sighed. He'd never imagined he would ever be in a situation where there would be a literal *line* of girls waiting to be married to him. As a man, he should have rather liked his situation, but all he felt was a hollow sort of pang in his chest.

Alyssa pouted, breaking him out of his reverie. "David," she asked, voice tight, and brittle, "if you get married, does that mean we have to share you?"

Victoria and Anna instantly abandoned their letter opening and looked up expectantly. With three tiny, identically expectant faces looking up at him, he couldn't help but laugh.

"No ladies," he said, quick to reassure them. "It just means that I would have to share *you*."

❧

By THE END OF WEEK THREE, WITH A CONSTANT running commentary from his sisters and quiet insight from Albert, he had lined up three candidates for a final interview. It felt like his life was hanging by a thread, and if he made the wrong call, then it was going to wither away and he'd fall.

A day after, he received one last application. It came in a

sad looking envelop, and when he read the letter inside, he couldn't help but be appalled. He would have instantly crumpled up the paper, thrown it in the bin, and gone on with business, had a sepia photograph not fallen out of the envelop and Victoria not jumped three feet like a cat to grab at it.

"Oh!" she exclaimed after carefully examining it for all of two seconds. "Oh, David!"

Curious, David crouched down and took his first look. He blinked. The woman in the photograph was smirking rather smugly, as if to taunt him after the kind of letter she'd sent him. But aside from the smirk, she was... quite exquisite, he had to admit.

Even in the brown of the photograph, he could make out the platinum of her hair, the light of her eyes, and some very cutting cheekbones.

"Oh, David!" Victoria whispered. "She looks like a princess."

She did.

But she sounded like a criminal.

"Ahan," he said, gingerly taking away the photograph and placing it in his desk drawer, then crumpling up the letter and throwing it in the bin.

Had he been careful enough, he would have noticed the gleam in Victoria's eyes. Had he had enough foresight, he would have set contingencies against his sisters entering his office. Had he been wise, he would have known that all three of those little menaces would strong arm Albert into writing a response.

But all he had been was very, very tired.

So he retired to his room and instantly fell asleep, never even imagining that things would get so out of hand.

$ 6 $

WHEN MARY GOT A LETTER CONTAINING A TIME AND place for an interview, she was appropriately appalled. She slowly pulled down the letter and stared at nothing in particular. Her heart beat hollowly in her chest.

Pa, on the other hand, had been ecstatic, had even shed a few tears of joy, then promptly tired himself out and fallen back in bed.

"Ye' did well, child," he told her before succumbing to sleep.

Except she *hadn't* done well. She'd been obscene and reckless and – she didn't understand *why* someone like David Griffin would want to see a con like her.

Maybe it had been curiosity that had dragged her to the Griffin Estate on the requisite day, donned in her best gown and made up in the best of all that she owned. A strangely dressed old man had showed her to a parlor where two other women waited.

They looked jittery and nervous, and Mary felt bad for

them because all she felt was a twitching sort of annoyance.

One by one the ladies were called in, and then bounced out looking appropriately doozy, making her wonder what exactly went on inside that room. When it was her turn, the call came a bit later than expected, and she had to wonder if David Griffin had suddenly changed his mind. It made her bristle and grit her teeth.

She stood up, fully intending to storm out of the immaculate looking parlor, but when she whirled around there were two young girls standing in her path.

She blinked.

"Hello," they said in unison.

"Uh," she replied, not quite coherent, because those girls looked eerily alike. Same height, same red hair, same shy smiles, and when another one took her place beside the other two, Mary blinked in surprise and wondered if she was actually dreaming.

"You're really, *really* pretty," said one of them, stepping out of line and leaning close to her. She looked around the age of five, maybe six years old, tiny and uncannily adorable, and suddenly Mary felt very scared.

That foreboding only intensified when there was a creak from behind and a head peeked out. She could only assume it was David Griffin because the girls suddenly stood at attention and looked at him with wide, adoring eyes.

David coughed. "Miss Mary Brown?"

"Yes."

He opened the door wider, and she could finally see his tall frame. "Please, come inside."

She opened her mouth to refuse, because now that

she'd seen he was tall, built, very handsome, and extremely wealthy – and came with three tiny daughters that hadn't been mentioned in the ad – she had no desire to waste her breath or time on this.

But apparently things were out of her hand, because suddenly she was being shuffled along to the room by the hem of her skirts by three small propellers. "C'mon!" they urged her.

And she stumbled away to her doom.

WHEN DAVID FIRST SAW MARY BROWN'S CARD SITTING in tandem with the rest of the women he'd called out, he'd felt a numb sort of shock. By the time he'd shaken it off, the tea in his cup had become cold. Albert, who had been acting as a chaperone between him and the ladies, looked distinctly uncomfortable, and suddenly David remembered the excited gleam in Victoria's eyes the night before.

He sighed, because things suddenly made a lot more sense. His sisters were mischievous little rascals, and now he didn't know what to make of an already awkward situation.

He cleared his throat. "Is she here?"

Albert seemed to know who he was referring to. "Yes, Sir."

David pinched the bridge of his nose and inhaled sharply. He didn't know whether to call for her or not. She'd been brutally honest in her letter, and by this time she must have been thinking he was some shameless pervert.

He wasn't.

He was just… he didn't know.

"May I call her in?"

He didn't know. He couldn't decide. He wondered what would he say. What *should* he say?

"Sir?"

But she'd come, hadn't she? No matter her circumstances, she'd come, and he owed it to her to at least see her once.

So, he got up and stumbled to the door, Albert on his heels.

When he opened the door, he saw what he'd been dreading all along. The triplets, in full confine and define mode, were holding her captive in their small, three-way circle.

He cleared his throat. "Miss Mary Brown?"

She turned, looking like a deer caught in the woods, and not at all the mean, black hearted con artist she'd portrayed herself to be. "Yes."

Against all better judgment, he said, "Please, come inside."

And his sisters herded her in.

🙚🙘

To say that the situation was awkward would have been an understatement. The silence was thick with palpable tension as Albert poured them a fresh cup of tea each. The triplets looked like a bunch of cats who'd caught a nest full of canaries, and Mary seemed like she'd rather be anywhere but there.

He cleared his throat.

Albert took the cue. "I believe it is time for your naps,

young misses."

All three of them groaned. "Aw, but can't we stay just this once?"

Albert changed tactics. "I believe your brother would like some time alone with the young Miss."

They all cleared out in record time. David knew they'd all be listening at the door, and motioned for Albert to play security guard.

When they were finally alone, Mary Brown turned to him. "Ye' have three sisters?"

"Yes."

"An' ye' expect yer' wife te' take care of 'em?"

"Certainly."

She snorted.

He took a sip of his tea. "You're rather eccentric, Miss Brown."

She shrugged.

"Your letter was rather intriguing."

She shrugged again.

"You seem to have done some obscene things."

She didn't look away. Instead, she nodded. "I did what I had te' do."

"And you had to con people, because...?"

"That's the only way I know how to live."

She didn't stutter, but she did blink, and his heart ached for her. While she'd been brutally honest about what she was, there must have been circumstances that had made her that way.

"I need a wife who I can entrust my sisters to. Why do you think you're capable of that?"

She scowled. "I'm not."

He leaned back, surprised and amused. "Then are you

here to con me?"

She smirked. "You wish."

He almost smiled. "Then why do you wish to be my wife?"

"Because my Pa is dyin' and it's his last will an' testament, apparently."

She was so candid, and so matter-of-fact in her speech, but in her eyes he could see a deep heartache that never showed on the impassivity of her face.

"So you plan to throw away your free will because your father demands it of you?"

Her brow twitched, then furrowed. He seemed to have been getting under her skin. "I am doin' no such thing," she told him patiently.

"Did you send me a letter full of your ugly deeds so I wouldn't accept your proposal?"

"Yes."

He nodded. She was clever and beautiful and slightly mad. She was being deliberately truthful, and where he should have been utterly appalled, he found himself being incessantly intrigued. He wanted to say he would take her as his wife just to see how shocked she would be, but marriage was a commitment of a lifetime, and his sister's education and upbringing was at stake.

So, he said, "You may take your leave."

She seemed to bristle at his curt dismissal, but then got up and stomped out.

THAT NIGHT, ANNA FOUND HIM SITTING ON THE SMALL balcony attached to his room. She was tired and sleepy, and apparently very curious. "David?" she said, tugging at his pants and raising her arms to be swung on his lap.

He obliged her. "Yes?"

"Are you going to marry that pretty lady?"

"No, sweetheart."

"Why?"

"She's... she's not very conventional."

Anna snuggled into his embrace. "What's '*conventional*'?"

David rocked her in his arms. "Um, ordinary?"

"But isn't that a good thing?"

Any other day, he would have agreed with her, but Mary was as dangerous as she was unconventional.

"Anna?"

"Hmm?"

"What do you think I should do?"

"Mmm, I think you should choose the princess."

"Why?"

"Because she seems like she needs a prince."

❆   7   ❆

SOMETIMES HAVING A SERIOUS CONVERSATION WITH A five-year-old seemed to put things in perspective. Out of all the women he'd shortlisted, one came with a child of her own, one was definitely hawking out for his wealth, and the last one was not exactly as she'd defined herself to be. Of what he'd seen of this American community, there was a lot of desperation, and the need for some monetary recognition was a bit too assimilated.

Even if he looked a thousand miles away, he knew that he was never going to find someone he would be completely satisfied with – always on the edge, fraught with imagined dooms.

Mary Brown was clearly a desperate woman who'd taken the wrong path somewhere down the road of life and didn't know the way back.

And as Anna had so eloquently put it, she seemed like she needed a prince.

As he had Albert draft up the marriage contract, and

later put his seal on it, he prayed to God that he was doing the right thing.

⚜

THE ONLY THING SHE COULD THINK ABOUT AS THE carriage trotted towards the Griffin Estate was that this was karma finally catching up to her. She had taken away so much from so many innocent people, and this was God's retribution. Her eyes stung with tears, but she refused to shed them.

If only it hadn't been Pa who'd opened the mail that day. If only he hadn't looked so happy. If only her heart was cold enough to refute his last request.

She'd looked into Pa's eyes, which had sparkled just like they used to back when Ma had been with them, alive and wide and gleaming with happy tears. Even his matted beard had seemed to magically clear itself of the dirt.

Mary had completely lost the will to refute when he'd taken her hands and said, very wetly, very thickly, "Thank ye'."

Then she'd put her seal on the contract and signed away her life.

⚜

IT WAS ALBERT, THE BUTLER, WHO OPENED THE DOOR for her when she arrived.

Instantly, she was heralded by three raging red thunderstorms.

"You're here!"

"He chose you!"

"I'm *so* happy!"

She didn't even have time to blink. All she could do was look down in a daze as David's sisters took her by the fluff of her skirt and dragged her in.

"Young ladies," Albert the butler chided gently. "Must you give our guest a hard time?"

"But she's not a guest!" piped up one of the girls.

"She's our sister now!" another one shot back, sticking her tongue out.

Albert sighed, and Mary could do nothing but be dragged away by the little girls because her mind was reeling and her throat was constricting with panic and fear. She wanted to back up and run away, but her legs wouldn't work on their own. The only thing she could actually do was be herded wherever the girls were taking her.

HE FOUND HER SQUATTING BESIDE THE GIRLS, LOOKING desperately out of place and on the brink of running away. He stood by the door and observed, though did nothing to pluck her out of that situation. He wanted to see if she would break, crack under the pressure of the hurricanes that were his sisters and do something that would show her self-proclaimed and inherently vile nature.

For ten minutes, he stood at the jamb.

"Will you have tea parties with us?"

"Please?"

"Pretty, please?"

"Albert doesn't let us have actual tea, but sometimes we sneak in water."

"Mrs. Hamlet likes it very much."

"Mrs. Hamlet is her bunny."

"How is your hair so pretty?"

"How long did it take you to grow it out?"

"Whoa, your eyes look like the jade stone David keeps in his drawer."

"No, they look like the plants."

"That's not romantic at all."

"Are you alright? You look a little strange."

"See, you made her mad!"

"She's not mad! Are you?"

The barrage of questions, observations, and childlike invitations kept coming, and Mary Brown seemed to be drowning under the deluge. He wanted to smile when she buried her head in her arms, maybe to block away the world, or maybe to get a hold of her new reality.

But then Victoria brushed at her hair, and suddenly she was up and backing away, looking like she was about to be hit by a freight train, and David knew he had to intervene.

"Girls," he said and clapped his hands once. The triplets seemed to line up, and from the corner of his eye, he could see Mary looking wild and frantic.

Alyssa stepped out, all innocent blinking and serene smiles. "Yes, David?"

David shook his head in amused redundancy and motioned for Mary to join him. "I'll be taking your new toy. I do believe it's time for a nap."

They groaned in unison, and there was a relieved slump to Mary's shoulders when she joined him at the door.

"We'll be seeing you at breakfast tomorrow."

"I'M SORRY ABOUT THAT," HE SAID, AND MARY TURNED to look at him. He was smiling softly, and she wanted to commit an act of violence against him.

"Sorry about what?" she asked just to spite him.

He shrugged. "I know my sisters can be a handful."

Mary almost shuddered, but then remembered that she was an adult, these girls were just pesky little children, and she needed to take command of the situation. So, she said, "I'm glad that you're aware."

He led her down the parlor to the main hall, and out into a sprawling garden that spread in the wake of his home. It was strange and unconventional. The only gardens Mary had ever seen in the area were small patches of brown grass that never thrived. She wanted to ask him about it, but didn't. Instead, she asked, "Where are ye' goin?"

He only half turned back. "It's a beautiful evening. I wanted to enjoy it."

It was pure horse puckey, and he knew it. He wanted her to start the conversation, and she refused to be manipulated. Stubbornly, she grit her teeth and remained silent as they walked past immaculately manicured grass and thriving rose bushes.

He must have sensed that he wasn't going to get anywhere because he abruptly turned around and peered at her face.

She cringed back. It made her uncomfortable. "What?" she snapped, and he replied with a soft half smile.

"Nothing. Just looking for the hardened criminal you've rendered yourself to be."

She would have growled if her pride would have let her. "I will suck every penny of yer' estate dry."

He leaned back and turned around, then started walking again. "I would very gladly like to see you do that, and sneak it past my sisters. As you've witnessed firsthand, they are quite the menaces."

She wholeheartedly agreed, but would have stabbed herself with the largest kitchen knife she could find before ever admitting it out loud.

He led her around the garden twice, then walked her back to her allocated room.

"I will see you tomorrow," he said before slightly bowing his head and walking away.

She stared at his back for five heartbeats before loudly slamming the door and striding to the bed. She didn't change out of her skirts, just lay on the bed, stared at the ceiling, and dreaded the next day to come.

MARY HAD LURED A HERD OF INNOCENT LADS TO THEIR doom. She was used to smiling in uncomfortable situations, playing coy, and getting what she wanted. She might have even tried that on David, except she never quite had the chance.

Victoria, Alyssa, and Anna, the treasure train of doom, were strangely attracted to her, and she, in turn, was strangely terrified of them.

Each time one of them came in close range, all she could think about was fleeing and never looking back. Maybe it was the expectations that had come with this marriage, that David essentially wanted a caretaker for his siblings, and she was nowhere capable enough to be that. Or maybe it had been the adoring eyes that followed her every move.

Years and years of being alone had taught her that depending on people was bad, but having people depend on you – especially tiny little human things like the triplets – was even worse. She remembered how kind her Ma had been, how devastated she'd been when she'd passed away, and how it had led to the deterioration of her life.

Whenever the three of them looked at her, she was reminded of the time she looked exactly like that at her own mother, and she was terrified of being that person to them.

❧

"IT'S FUNNY," SAID DAVID, ONE BLESSED DAY WHEN THE girls were being tutored.

"What?" she snapped, but the sting in the word was almost neutral now. She didn't know when, but she'd surrendered herself to this fate. She suspected it had happened somewhere between the umpteenth tea party and the princess play.

"You're scared of three little girls who adore you."

She took a deep breath. "I'm not scared o' anythin'."

David hid his smile behind a cup of tea. "Whatever you say, dear."

She ground her teeth and bit savagely into her bread. David had taken to calling her 'dear', and at first she'd been too shocked to say anything. She thought it might be a temporary thing, as making Mary uncomfortable seemed to be David's favorite pastime, and just assumed it would go away.

But 'dear' had become an endearing habit, and maybe because she had actually protested – "Stop calling me that!" – or maybe because it was actually starting to grow on him, but he'd started using it more, perhaps just to spite her.

Whatever the reason, it now made her heart flutter.

The last time Mary's heart had fluttered, some rich old lady had thrown a glass full of ice cold water in her face.

She did not want to relive that.

So, she grit her teeth and desperately tried to ignore each time he uttered the endearment.

***

VICTORIA WAS THE ONE WITH THE LONG HAIR. SHE WAS the most mischievous of the bunch, and more often than not acted as the leader of their naughty shenanigans. Once Mary had caught her climbing up a tall ladder of her sister's bodies to get at the cookie jar, and scrambled to catch her when that plan had inevitably failed. Her small body had fit perfectly against Mary's front, and the grin she'd flashed up at her after had almost make her heart melt. Mary had looked into those big, brown eyes and wanted to hold her closer.

She'd been so scared at the notion that her heart had pounded after, as Albert had gently chastised the 'little madams'.

She'd closed herself in the room for the rest of the night and refused to have dinner.

***

ALYSSA WAS THE CHEEKY ONE WITH FRECKLES UNDER her nose and a smile that was slightly wider than her other two counterparts. She liked to crack jokes and have tea parties with her stuffed doll Mrs. Hamlet, and constantly invited her to 'secret' parties, which were just a round table fixed with several stuffed toys in the cellar. Mary never accepted her invitations, and felt a pang in her chest every time she didn't have the courage to do so.

But one day, while she was searching for the cooking pot, she'd accidentally stumbled into the cellar, where Alyssa had paused to look at her with a plastic tea cup held at David's lips.

She'd blinked, once, twice, and had resisted the urge to laugh at David, who'd crouched himself to fit at the small table, and now looked horrified to have been caught by her, of all people.

"Mary!" Alyssa had cried. "You came!"

And Mary had broken right out of her hilarious reverie, quickly protesting, "No, I jus'–"

She hadn't even been allowed to complete her unceremonious denial before being shoved by a surprisingly strong armed little Alyssa into a chair right next to David's. So surprised had she been by the turn of events that she'd hadn't had the mind to deny the cup that was pressed into her hands.

It was only when Alyssa took her seat that Mary finally realized what was happening. She was being sucked into this vortex, where tiny humans and ridiculous shenanigans were a constant reminder of how far off base she'd come.

Suddenly feeling suffocated, she'd been about to shoot up, run away, and lock herself in her room again, when David had put his hand on her arm. She'd been so startled by the impromptu touch that she'd forgotten how to speak.

David had passed her a quiet smile and raised the cup to his lips.

Taking cue from his movements, she'd done the same, feeling her heart pounding in her chest.

"Pie?" Alyssa had offered, and Mary had found herself chomping on thin air as a pretense for delicious pies.

When the party had been wrapped up, and the guests dismissed, she hadn't instantly recoiled when Alyssa had taken her by the hand and made her walk side by side with David.

⚜

ANNA WAS THE WISE ONE. COMPARED TO HER SISTERS, she was quiet, though especially gullible. She'd once caught Victoria urging her to eat a mud pie for fun, and had barely had time to run over and smack her in the back when she'd started to choke. It had taken three minutes to clear her throat, and Mary's heart had galloped in her chest so hard she'd been afraid it would run out and splay all her organs onto the ground.

Anna had been so exhausted after that Mary had had to carry her inside in her arms, and when Albert had tried to take her away, she'd stubbornly clung on. David had thoroughly chastised Victoria, and Anna had refused to talk to her for a week after.

But that night, when she'd been lying awake, ruminating over the course her life had taken, how she was slowly, but surely, against all better judgment, getting attached to the girls, there had been a knock on the door.

Expecting Albert, she'd opened the door only to find Anna standing outside, looking hopeful and teary up at her.

She'd stood at the door for a full minute, wavering about letting her in or sending her away, when Anna had slid past her skirt and run onto her bed.

For some reason, Mary had felt tears sting at her eyes as she'd closed the doors and come inside, felt her chest ache with something unfathomable when Anna had patted the space beside herself, and her jaw had clenched when she'd sat down beside her.

After an eternity of silence, she'd found herself asking, "Are ye' better now?"

Anna had nodded. "Are you?" she'd asked, blinking with childlike innocence, and Mary had felt her heart give.

"Why wouldn't I be?" she'd asked.

"Because," Anna had replied. "You're not conventional."

❄   9   ❄

SHE WAS THAWING. DAVID COULD SEE THAT IN A million tiny things. Mary Brown's frigid heart was slowly melting.

There was hesitation now in everything that she did. Hesitation of the impact that things might have on the girls.

He saw it in the careful selection of her cook pots. How her gravy was just the right mix of salt and spice, because once Victoria had choked on the aftertaste when she'd first tried her hand at it.

He saw it in her careful supervision of Anna. She'd been terrified when she'd swallowed a load of mud, and had been sick for days after.

He saw it in her ginger participation in Alyssa's secret tea parties. How she was slowly starting to pay more attention to the toys, how she was adapting to the silly etiquettes that Alyssa liked to impose, and how she would hide her smile by averting her head to the side when she found something ridiculous or funny.

But most of all, he saw it in the careful restraint of her eyes when she met his gaze, or caught him staring. The small upturn on her lips when he called her 'dear', and her constant rebuttal of everything he said to her, which now completely lacked the venom and sting of their previous encounters.

She was acclimating to them, and they to her. Her lazy drawl was growing on him, and every time a long strand of hair fell on her face, he wanted to be the one who tucked it away behind her ear.

He thought that if he wasn't careful, he might end up actually falling for her.

❧

PA DIED EXACTLY SIX MONTHS AFTER SHE GOT MARRIED. She received the news via mail, and was so devastated that she fell to her knees on the front stairs and could not move a muscles. Maybe it was shock, maybe it was grief, but she found that she couldn't let out a single tear. Her mouth refused to open, and her eyes refused to blink. After several billion years, and an eternity, David finally came and sat beside her.

For a moment, he didn't say anything, didn't do anything. Then, he'd held out his hand and asked, "May I?"

She still couldn't move, couldn't speak, and when he gently pried the letter away from her, she couldn't resist.

"Oh, Mary," he sighed when he'd read the contents. Without further ado, he put an arm around her shoulders.

She broke then. Something inside of her must have shattered, because what else could explain how she completely broke down and clung to him, how she wailed and cried and sniffled, and when all the tears had dried and she could finally breath again, she realized that he'd been holding her. He was holding her up, and she would have fallen a long time ago if he hadn't plucked her from the middle of nowhere and put her in the right place at the right time.

David Griffin, along with her Pa, had saved her from herself, and she didn't know how she was ever going to repay their kindness.

❦

THE GIRLS CAME TO HER THAT NIGHT, LOOKING LIKE SAD puppies, and this time she didn't hesitate to open her door wider. They trudged in one after the other, and without permission, made themselves comfortable in her bed.

She sat down beside them.

"We heard," said Victoria, gentle, and tentative. "Your Papa passed away."

Mary's lip wobbled, and Alyssa jumped up and threw her arms around her. Mary didn't hesitate to return the hug. It was warm and comforting, and she needed all the comfort that she could in that moment. It wasn't long before Victoria and Anna wrapped themselves around her too.

"It's okay, Mary," they told her. "Our Papa passed away too."

"David says he's in a better place."

And suddenly Mary was crying again, because there was so much kindness and love in their words, and their arms, and their bodies, and she felt like she deserved none of it. But she hugged them back anyway and remembered how she used to hold God's words close to her heart when she was little too.

Let all that you do, be in love.

She wondered when had she stopped loving.

Where had she gone wrong?

So, she let the girls hug her, and held them close, and she didn't know when, or how they fell asleep like that, but when she opened her eyes next, the sun was peeking in from the window, and there was a small huddle of tiny bodies sleeping around her.

Her heart felt just a little less bruised that day.

DAVID WAS TALL AND LEAN AND HANDSOME, AND WHEN he looked at her with those piercing blue eyes, her heart always, *always* fluttered these days. But that was not the only gesture that would make her heart flutter. It lit up like a warm pyre in the middle of a wintery cold every time he called her 'dear', and roared like a raging fire every time his hand would accidentally brush against her.

She didn't know what to make of it.

"But that just means that he's your prince," Anna told her one day.

"What de' ye mean, sweetheart?"

Anna rolled her eyes dramatically. She must have picked that up from Victoria, Mary mused.

"It means that you kind of love him," Alyssa contributed, running a hand through Mary's hair and saying such huge words with such nonchalance that it took Mary a few minutes to actually comprehend their meaning.

"What?"

Victoria took that as a cue to sidle up in her lap. "You're very pretty."

"Thank you."

"David thinks you're pretty, too."

"Oh."

"You think David is pretty too, right?"

"I... um..."

"That just means you two like each other."

Mary didn't know how to respond to that.

❧

IN RETROSPECT, SHE KNEW THAT SHE DID *RESPECT* David. He was a fine man with loft standards, and he'd taken a huge chance with her. But... *love?*

The last time Mary had thought about falling in love, she'd gotten a face full of disappointment and bitter words. She didn't want that again.

But she also knew that her circumstances were different now. That her heart was not a closed off vagabond waiting to run to the next destination, fighting for survival in a cruel world.

She had Victoria, who was a little too sassy for an almost six year old, and she had Alyssa, who was a mischievous brat, and she had Anna, who was wise beyond her years.

And she had David, who had caught her in a path lined with pointy thorns and led her to a field of daisies instead. Maybe, she thought, her shriveled coal of a heart was coming alive again.

❦ 10 ❧

HE COULD FEEL THE CHANGE. IT WASN'T INSTANT, BUT IT was there in her tiny smiles and her hesitant touch. He'd taken to holding her hand when they took their daily stroll through the gardens. He liked seeing the moonlight reflect off her hair, the cut of her cheeks, the glint in her eyes.

But before moving any further, he wanted to know her just a little bit more.

"Thank you," he said one night.

"Fer' what?"

He grinned, wanting her to understand that he was about to make a joke so she shouldn't take offence. "For not robbing me blind."

Three months ago, she would have either kicked him in the shin, or completely closed off and run away. Today, she smirked at him and said, "Yer' lucky I like yer' sisters."

"What about me?" he asked.

Her expression shuttered, then flickered to shy, and his heart pounded because if Mary was being shy, then that meant she felt the same.

"Am I right?" he asked, feeling hopeful.

She averted her face, and just when he thought she wouldn't answer him, she whipped around and admitted, "Yes. Maybe. I dunno. Yes?"

He laughed, because Mary stuttering was something new and amazing, and he wanted to tuck this moment away in his heart and never let it go. She blushed and looked away, but when he laced his fingers through hers, she didn't shake him off.

They strolled around the pavers, and in the magic of the moment, he told her about his lineage, about how he'd been carted off to America. How his father had been assassinated, and how, sometimes, he desperately missed his home.

She squeezed his hand, and her answer both surprised and amused him.

"I'm glad they shipped ye' here. Who else would'a saved me?"

He couldn't help but smile, because he was glad he'd been the one to save her.

They took a second route, and when they returned home, she sat him down on the porch.

"I don't wanna deal with those girls, jus' yet."

"I completely understand, my dear."

So, they sat in comfortable silence for a while, and after they'd watched the moon make adequate progress across the sky, she turned to him, and in her eyes was the truth. She was completely unguarded in that moment, and he thought he'd never seen anyone so exquisite and so beautiful, and he would forever carry her next words in his heart.

"I think I love you."

"I think I love you very much too, my dear."

EPILOGUE

1 YEAR LATER

"Nooo!"

"Yesss!"

"I agree a little bit with both of them."

Mary smirked. "I thought you'd be *excited*."

"But... but I'm *seven*! I'm too young to be an aunt!" Victoria cried.

David sighed out a laugh and rubbed a hand at her back.

"Does this mean we get new clothes?" Alyssa inquired.

"Could I sleep with the baby when it's born?" asked Anna.

"Is it a boy or a girl?"

"Oh, I hope it's a girl!"

"It's gonna be a boy."

"No! Boys are icky!"

"*You're* icky!"

"Girls," said David firmly, and all of them turned around with rapt attention. "I'm glad you're excited about having a new baby, but could you *please* tone it down?"

"Are you going to be mean to us now that you're having your own baby?"

"Never."

"Don' worry, girls," Mary said reassuringly. "I'll beat 'im up, if he's mean te' ye. Now go to your room. It's time fer' bed."

The girls gave her a proverbial salute and skittered away. Beside her, David sighed.

"That was hard."

"I think it went better than we could have imagined."

He held her close. "Since when did you become an optimist, my dear Mary?"

"Since I met my Englishman, David." She smiled, thanking God for her new chance at life, at family, and at making a new home.

☙❧

THERE WAS A NEW WING IN THE ESTATE NOW, ONE ON the west side with a full view to the gardens. When you stood on the main porch, you could watch the vast sprawl of green, the colorful tangle of the rose bushes. There were more now, a rainbow of red, yellow, pink, and orange.

Mary liked to believe that this wing had helped her toward her redemption. Each morning she stood at the edge of the garden and watched the sun rise, reflecting off the windows of Brown School for the Less Fortunate, and today, as she stood by the dahlias, David stood beside her.

"Feeling proud?" he asked with a soft smile.

"Feelin' relieved," she replied.

In a few hours there would be children lining the gates, studying, learning, playing, and running around. She would make her rounds, take inventory, and make sure the place was running like a well-oiled machine.

David pulled her closer. She leaned into him, and sighed. She felt like she'd finally repaid her debt, that she deserved the happiness of loving Victoria, Alyssa, Anna, and David, that being saved by them was not just a divine intervention, but a path that led to a bigger, brighter future where Mary Brown was not afraid to love or be loved.

To continue enjoying Bonanza Brides Find Prairie Love Series (13 Book.) Please check below

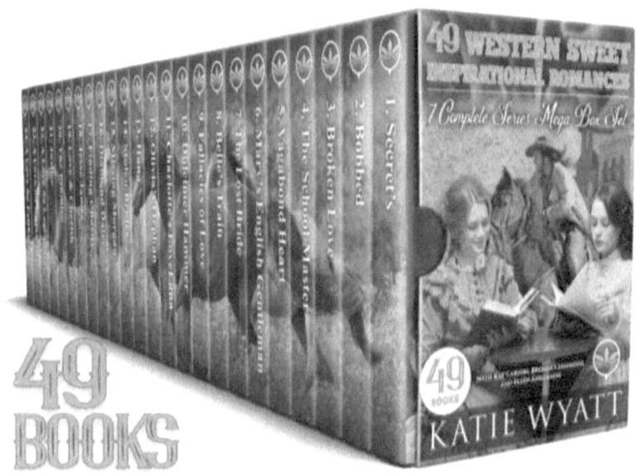

Katie Wyatt 49 Western Sweet inspirational Romances
mega box set

Recommended Reads others books Stories old and new from our library of love

katie wyatt kat carson love me love my dog western romance

ROYCE CARDIFF PUBLISHING HOUSE PRESENTS OTHER wonderful clean, wholesome and inspiring romance short stories titles for your entertainment. Many are value boxset and as always FREE to Kindle Unlimited readers.

Katie Wyatt Mega Box Set Series

COMPLETE SERIES
Sweet Western Romance

KATIE WYATT, BRENDA CLEMMONS AND ELLEN ANDERSON

katie wyatt box set complete series

Thank you so much for reading my book. I sincerely hope you enjoyed every bit reading it. I had fun creating it and will surely create more .

Your positive reviews are very helpful to other reader, it only takes a few moments. They can be left at Amazon.

https://www.amazon.com/Kat-Carson/e/B01G333YP0

Want free books every week? Who doesn't!

Become a preferred reader and we'll not only send you free reads, but you'll also receive updates about new releases.

So you'll be among the first to dive into our latest new books, full of adventure, heartwarming romances, and characters so real they jump off the page.

It's absolutely free and you don't need to do anything at all to qualify except click here.

PREFERRED READ FREE READS

https://katcarsonbooks.getresponsepages.com

ABOUT THE AUTHOR

Kat Carson lives in New Mexico with her two dogs, a horse, and 20 chickens. She started writing when she was a teenager and has never stopped. She loves the rich culture of the old West. Some of her stories are inspired by tales from the local storytellers in New Mexico and what her grandparents used to tell her. Others are when she travels around in her RV camping, fishing, hiking, climbing and engaging with other interesting people along the way.

She writes stories derived from actual historical facts and events and sometimes individuals with interesting characters in nature that will captivate you and leave you in awe with the twists and turns of every story. Packed with action, humor, challenge, and adventure her short stories will stretch the limits of your imagination, allowing you to marvel at the fascinating time in US history. I recommend them for anybody who enjoys an excellent feel good clean and wholesome romance story.